*For my parents*
~Alison

*For Nana & Auntie Mary*
~Joanne

**TED SMART**

This edition produced for
The Book People Ltd
Hall Wood Avenue, Haydock, St Helens WA11 9UL, by
LITTLE TIGER PRESS
1 The Coda Centre, 189 Munster Road, London SW6 6AW
First published in Great Britain 1998
Text © 1998 Alison Allen-Gray
Illustrations © 1998 Joanne Moss
Alison Allen-Gray and Joanne Moss have asserted their rights
to be identified as the author and illustrator of this work
under the Copyright, Designs and Patents Act, 1988.
Printed in Belgium by Proost NV, Turnhout
All rights reserved • ISBN 1 85430 472 0
1 3 5 7 9 10 8 6 4 2

# The Lost Kitten

by Alison Allen-Gray

illustrated by Joanne Moss

Kitten was happy living in the shed. She had Mum's soft fur to snuggle against, Mum's warm milk to drink and lots of flower pots to play in.

One night Mum said, "You need grown-up food now, Kitten."
"Like what?" asked Kitten.
"Dustbin scraps, or a juicy mouse," said Mum.
"Yuk!" said Kitten.
"Don't say Yuk! till you've tried them," said Mum.
"Now, I'm going out. Stay right here till I get back — promise?"
"Promise," said Kitten.
And Mum slunk out into the dark to look for food.

Kitten popped in and out of her pots.
She swiped at the spiders,
but they all pinged away.

She chased
a tail, but when
she caught it,
she found it
was hers.

Suddenly she felt lonely and
hungry. She wanted Mum's
soft fur and Mum's
warm milk.

Kitten forgot all about her
promise and crept out
into the dark to
look for Mum.

With her night-time eyes Kitten could see tall grass
and tangly bushes. With her night-time nose she
could smell rotting rubbish and damp dew. With her
night-time ears she could hear the squeaking and
scratching of other night-time animals.
But she couldn't see or smell or hear Mum.

And then she *did* see something – a shadow flapping
in the night sky.
"GET OUT OF THE WAY!" it screeched.

The shadowy thing
crashed into a bush.
It flapped and fluttered
and cried, "Clumsy idiot!"
"No, you're not!" said Kitten. "Anyone could
fall into a bush, especially in the dark."
"Not ME!" flapped Owl. "I mean clumsy YOU!
I was after a mouse, but you frightened it away."
"Sorry," said Kitten. "I only wanted
my mum!"
"And I only wanted my supper!"
screeched Owl.
"Now, GET LOST!"

Owl looked so feathery and
furious that Kitten
ran and ran . . .

. . . until she *was* lost.
And then she smelt something —
a scrumptious sausage!
Kitten put out a paw . . .

. . . and something said, "GGGRRRR!
Touch that sausage and you're in BIG TROUBLE,"
snarled Dog. He snatched the sausage, and spat it
out again. "Hoooo, Haaaa, Hoooo – Hhhot!"
"Careful," said Kitten. "You'll burn your tongue!"

"I hab burred by
bung!" said Dog.
The sausage
began to roll.
It rolled and
rolled . . .

. . . straight down a drain.
"MY SAUSAGE!" howled Dog.
"Sorry," said Kitten. "I only wanted my mum!"
"And I only wanted my sausage!" said Dog.
"Now, GET LOST!"
Dog looked so snappy and snarly
that Kitten ran and ran . . .

. . . until she was even *more* lost.
And now she could hear something
rustling in a dustbin.
"Mum?" squeaked Kitten.

"Do I look like your
mum?" said Rat,
popping out his head.
"No," said Kitten. "My mum's pretty."
"Don't get smart with me, fluff-brain," sneered Rat.
"But I only want – " began Kitten.
"To pinch my supper!" snapped Rat.
"Well, PAWS OFF!"
The dustbin began to tip.
It tipped and
tumbled . . .

. . . straight into the canal.
"MY SUPPER!" wailed Rat.

Kitten didn't wait to
be told to get lost this time.
Rat looked so mad with rage that
Kitten ran and ran . . .

. . . until she was
*so* lost that she
thought she would
never ever find Mum.

And then she saw
something jumping
in the shadows.
A crisp packet!
"Mum?" mieowed Kitten.
"Is that you?"

The crisp packet began to tremble.

It trembled and trembled until . . .

"Hello," said Kitten.
"A juicy mouse!"
"No, I'm not!"
squeaked Mouse.
"I'm all skin
and bones,
honest! I hardly
get *anything* to eat."
"Neither do I," said Kitten sadly.
"Oh dear," said Mouse. "Have a crisp."
"Thanks," said Kitten. "Have you seen my mum?"
"No, thank goodness," said Mouse. "I know she's your mum, but
it's just that some cats *eat* mice – but only if they're desperate."
"*I'll* never eat you –
promise," said Kitten.
"Thanks," said Mouse.
And then he said,
"Listen!"

Kitten stopped crunching her crisps.
Mouse shook until his bones rattled inside his skin.
Pawsteps on the roof!
"It's coming to eat me," he whimpered.
"Oh no it isn't," cried Kitten. "I'll look after you."

And she puffed up her fur and yelled,
"TOUCH THIS MOUSE AND YOU'RE IN BIG
TROUBLE, FLUFF-BRAIN. NOW, GET LOST!"
Silence.
Then the roof creaked and something said . . .

"DON'T SPEAK
TO YOUR
MOTHER LIKE THAT!"
Kitten got a big telling off
for going out on her own.
"Something *awful* could have
happened to you," said Mum.
"It nearly did," said Kitten. "I'm sorry, Mum."
But they were so glad to see each other, that Mum
forgave her. "Come on, there's lots to eat
at home," she said.
"Great!" cried Kitten. "I'm starving."
"Well then," said Mum, "why don't you eat this
measly mouse?"
"NO!" cried Kitten. "He's my friend and you
don't eat a friend, even if you're
desperate."

So Mum and Kitten invited Mouse back to supper.
On the way home Kitten thought about Owl and
Dog and Rat. She hoped that they'd found something
else to eat, but she needn't have worried . . .

. . . THEY HAD!